Adventure
to the

EIGHT WONDERS OF THE WORLD

COPY 2

by Carole Marsh

20 Years Ago . . .

As a mother and an author, one of the fondest periods of my life was when I decided to write mystery books for children. At this time (1979) kids were pretty much glued to the TV, something parents and teachers complained about the way they do about web surfing and blogging today.

I decided to set each mystery in a real place—a place kids could go and visit for themselves after reading the book. And I also used real children as characters. Usually a couple of my own children served as characters, and I had no trouble recruiting kids from the book's location to also be characters.

Also, I wanted all the kids—boys and girls of all ages—to participate in solving the mystery. And, I wanted kids to learn something as they read. Something about the history of the location. And I wanted the stories to be funny. That formula of real+scary+smart+fun served me well.

I love getting letters from teachers and parents who say they read the book with their class or child, then visited the historic site and saw all the places in the mystery for themselves. What's so great about that? What's great is that you and your children have an experience that bonds you together forever. Something you shared. Something you both cared about at the time. Something that crossed all age levels—a good story, a good scare, a good laugh!

20 years later,
Carole Marsh

Christina "Mystery Girl" Mimi Papa Grant

Hey, kids! As you see, here we are ready to embark on another of our exciting Carole Marsh Mystery adventures. My grandchildren often travel with me all over the world as I research new books. We have a great time together, and learn things we will carry with us for the rest of our lives!

I hope you will go to www.carolemarshmysteries.com and explore the many Carole Marsh Mysteries series!

Well, the Mystery Girl is all tuned up and ready for "take-off!" Gotta go...Papa says so! Wonder what I've forgotten this time?

Happy "Armchair Travel" Reading,

Mimi

About the Characters

Ms. Bogus' Fourth Grade
Alpine McAlpine School

Can you imagine a class where you go on field trips that are literally "out of this world?" The kids in Ms. Bogus' fourth grade class don't just imagine Fantasy Field Trips—they experience them!

Meet Ms. Bogus, the quirky teacher with the big heart and even bigger imagination! On the left are twins Skylar and Drew, and Colette, who sits in a wheelchair but stands tall in the middle of every Fantasy Field Trip adventure! On the right are Lucia, the girl who loves to travel; Willy, the class clown with lots of big ideas; and Sarah, the shy blonde who loves to read.

There are lots of other kids to meet in Ms. Bogus' class, too. So, let's go—it's time for a Fantasy Field Trip!

Books in This Series

#1 Adventure to the Eight Wonders of the World

#2 Adventure to the Planet Mars

#3 Adventure to the Pioneer Prairie

Table of Contents

Prologue

"What do you think of Ms. Bogus?" Sarah asked. Sarah was the tallest girl in the fourth grade at Alpine McAlpine School. Her sapphire eyes had a way of mesmerizing people when she talked.

"I don't know!" Lucia said. As she turned quickly toward Sarah, her dark, curly hair jiggled. "She seems okay, but I've heard strange things about her from some of the kids that had her last year."

"Strange things?" Sarah said. "What do they mean by *strange*? Is she a **clairvoyant** or does she talk to herself?"

"No," Lucia replied, "at least I don't think so. She lives by herself with a houseful of cats and wears those weird cat-eye glasses. They say she likes to go to the ballet and the opera by herself."

"Hmm!" Sarah said. "You should like her then. You're the one who loves to dance and do all that physical stuff."

"Well," Lucia said, "we can't all be star pupils. You need to get your head out of your books and come to a dance class with me. You'd love it!"

"You know I'm not very athletic," Sarah said. "I'm uncoordinated," she added, and changed the subject. "I really kind of like Ms. Bogus. She's strange to look at, but I get this feeling she genuinely cares about teaching."

Drew and his twin brother, Skylar, were sitting in the seats behind the girls. "You got the strange part right," Drew said. "She lives alone in a house filled with cats, and the only thing she ever eats is the tuna she feeds her cats."

"I heard she drives around in a really old pickup truck when she's not at school," Colette said, her hands resting on the wheels of her wheelchair. She sat across the aisle from Lucia and Sarah. "Some of the kids say she has cats buried all over her property and even in her basement!"

"Aw, that's nothing!" Skylar said, leaning forward in his seat. "I heard a story about Ms. B from a kid in sixth grade. He said that when she was younger, she went to prison for selling coats she made out of cat skins!"

Willy took a bite of a shiny, red apple. He sat across from the twins. "Man," he said, "you guys couldn't be any more wrong! Ms. B is the best teacher you'll ever have. She's nice, she's funny, and you can tell she likes to teach."

Willy's teeth crunched into his apple again. "So," he said, "as long as you're not a long-haired, furry cat, you have nothing to worry about!"

Spitball Maze

Sarah curled up in her usual position with her nose buried in a book. This time it was a book about the great wonders of the world. Everyone had to give an oral report on the wonder they'd love to visit. Sarah didn't want to visit any of them.

"I don't understand what people get out of traveling," Sarah said. "I'd rather see an atom split, or explore the chemical bonds between elements, or take a space trip to the moon or Mars. But to see a tower that's falling over? What's so great about that?"

Lucia looked up from the colorful travel book she was reading. "You crazy girl! I can't wait until I'm old enough to travel the world. I dream about spending my days lying on the beach in exotic places like Australia, New Zealand, or Brazil, or spending romantic nights in Rome or Paris."

Colette stuck a pink bookmark in her book about the Grand Canyon. "I'm not sure I'd want to travel to any of the world's wonders, either," Colette said, pushing a strand of red hair behind her ear, "although the Grand Canyon does seem fascinating."

A spitball splattered against Colette's book, just missing her hand. She saw a hand and straw disappear around the corner of a nearby bookshelf in the school library.

"Boys!" she hissed. "They just can't leave us alo—" A spitball smacked Lucia in the back of her head and another thumped against the stack of books in the middle of the table.

"Oh, boy!" Lucia said, pulling a couple of straws out of her backpack. "That's it! This is war!" She held the straws in the air. "Who's with me?"

"Where did you get those?" Colette asked.

"From the cafeteria," Lucia replied, wiggling her eyebrows. "I heard the boys talking about a spitball fight at lunch. My mom says a woman should never be caught off guard!"

"Let's teach them a lesson!" Colette cried, snatching a straw out of Lucia's hand.

Sarah cradled the book in her lap. "I've got to get ready for this report," she said. "You guys get them for me." But Lucia and Colette were already gone, vanishing into the maze of bookshelves around their table.

One For You, One For Me

Colette peeked between the books, scanning the aisles for the boys. She motioned to Lucia. "There they are," she whispered. The girls shifted quietly into position.

"Game over, boys!" Lucia and Colette shouted, as they launched their massive spitball attack.

The boys tried to dodge the **maelstrom** of spitballs, but simply couldn't avoid the barrage of wet, slimy pellets.

"Okay! Okay!" Willy and Drew shouted, their arms shielding their heads. "You win! You win!"

SWACK!

"Take that!" Colette said in an unusually loud voice.

SPLAT!

"And this!" Lucia added, and then suddenly yanked the straw out of her mouth and tucked it behind her back.

The boys saw her face and turned toward Colette, expecting to get hit with another spitball, but Colette's straw was nowhere in sight. Instead, Ms. Bogus was standing behind her.

"Hmm!" Ms. Bogus said. "Good shooting, girls, but as you said, 'Game's over!' It's time to go back to class." She started to turn, but stopped abruptly.

"Willy, Drew," Ms. Bogus said, "go clean the spitballs out of your hair. You'll be giving your oral reports first."

Tour Guide Lucia

Ms. Bogus stood at the front of the class. She was a tall, pear-shaped woman who was completely comfortable in her oversized dress, string of pearls, outdated slip-on shoes, and unbrushed, short haircut. She peered over the cat-eye glasses perched on the end of her pointy nose, scanning the room for the last person to present their report.

Skylar strolled back to his seat next to his brother after finishing his report. They were twins in every way, including their shaggy, sun-bleached, blond hair. The only way Ms. Bogus could tell them apart was by their eye color. Drew had intense, cobalt-blue eyes, while Skylar's eyes were kind of a puppy-dog, chocolate brown.

"Lucia," Ms. Bogus said. "It's your turn to give your report."

Lucia stood at the front of the class. "As you already know," Lucia said, "from everyone who did their report before me, the Grand Canyon is in the northern part of Arizona. It's 18 miles wide, 227 miles long, and about 5,000 feet deep. The Colorado River runs through the bottom of it.

"There are three cool things you can do at the Grand Canyon," she continued. "The first one is to take a burro ride from the top of the canyon all the way to the bottom of the canyon."

Willy lifted his straw and pretended to blow a spitball at Lucia. She jumped to her left to evade the spitball, which never came.

"The next cool thing," Lucia continued, glaring at Willy, "is to walk out on the Grand Canyon Glass Skywalk that the Hualapai Indians built." Lucia turned to the marker board and wrote the word 'Hualapai,' so the kids could see how to spell it.

"This thing is awesome!" Lucia reported. "It's 4,000 feet above the Colorado River, and juts 65 feet off the canyon rim into thin air. It has a glass bottom and can hold the weight of 71 fully loaded 747 airplanes."

"Seventy-one airplanes? Full of people?" Drew exclaimed. "That's unbelievable!"

"It's pretty amazing," Lucia agreed. "The skywalk can withstand winds up to 100 miles per hour from eight different directions and an 8.0 magnitude earthquake!"

Lucia smiled broadly. "But the coolest, most awesome thing to do," she added, "is to go whitewater rafting down the Colorado River. I went rafting on the Chattooga River in Georgia with my mom and it was incredibly scary and fun at the same time. I'd love to go rafting on the Colorado River!"

Lucia stacked her notecards neatly, signaling that her report was complete. "Although I picked the Grand Canyon as my favorite place to go," she continued, "I really want to travel around the whole world. My mom's a travel agent, so I read all the travel brochures she brings home."

"I want to stare up at the Leaning Tower of Pisa," a dark-haired boy in the back of the class said.

"I want to walk on the Great Wall of China," said a girl by the window.

"I want to play on the Giant's Causeway in Ireland," Drew said.

Willy tucked his straw in his pocket and stood up. "I want to stand at the top of the world on Mt. Everest and do a little dance like this." With his feet flying like a whirlwind, Willy danced up and down the aisle between the desks.

Everyone began to laugh and talk at the same time.

"Okay, class," Ms. Bogus said. "Quiet down and get back in your seats." She waited for the class to settle down. "So, all of you want to see the wonders of the world, do you?"

The children all nodded, except for Willy. A rare, serious look came over his freckled face. "That would be the coolest, Ms. B, but it wouldn't be any fun without you," he said.

"Good answer, Willy," Ms. Bogus remarked, with a chuckle. "Let me tell you what a trip to some of the wonders would be like. Everyone, clear off your desks, close your eyes, and relax. It's time to go on a field trip!

"But to get there, we're going to need transportation..."

Riddle Me This!

Drew felt something hard against his nose. He opened his eyes. His nose was pressed against the inside window of an airplane. He gawked at the houses and cars below, which from this altitude, looked as small as the bacteria he saw on the Petri dish in his science class this morning.

All of the other kids were peering out their own windows at the billowy white clouds against the azure blue horizon. "Ms. B," Drew asked, "how did we get on this airplane and what kind of airplane is it?"

"Drew, the 'how' is unimportant," Ms. Bogus said. "But this is a specially designed airplane I call the Jolly Jet. It allows us to fly in or out of the atmosphere, float or

dive under water, hover, ascend or descend in seconds, and zip us around faster than you'll ever believe!"

Ms. Bogus stood at the front of the plane and looked out into a sea of chattering faces. "Can I have your attention, please?" she said, as the children quieted down quickly.

"We are on the first leg of our first field trip," she said. "We have just enough time to see your eight favorite wonders of the world. I'm just not going to tell you where we're going first, or second, or third! Instead, I've decided to help you use your own reasoning powers to figure out where we are going.

"There will be a rhyming riddle hidden at each stop," Ms. Bogus continued. "You will need to solve the riddle before we, as a class, can move on to the next location."

"What if we're not good at riddles?" asked a tiny, blond girl in the back.

"Don't worry, dear," Ms. Bogus said. "Some of you will be better at this than

others, and that's okay, but it is **imperative** that you work together and help each other."

"We will be splitting into three groups of six," Ms. Bogus said. "If you look under your seat, you will see a card with your group's names on it."

Willy pulled out his card and smiled. "Hey, dudes," he said, looking at Drew and Skylar. "We're together with the girls."

Lucia whispered to Colette and Sarah. "This ought to be fun since we have those boys in our group."

"Oh, great," Colette said with a smile. "There goes the neighborhood."

"We can't ask to change partners?" Sarah teased.

"Don't get any ideas about changing partners," Ms. Bogus said. "These will be your partners in everything we do throughout the school year."

"I guess that answers my question," Sarah said.

"Hey," Lucia said, "it's only for the year."

"Have you ever walked around with a thorn in your side for a year?" Sarah asked. "It's painful. Very painful."

"Get in your groups," Ms. Bogus said. She removed a shiny metal tube from her dress pocket. She opened it, and a rolled-up piece of paper fell into her hand. She carefully unrolled the ancient-looking, cream-color scroll with burnt edges.

"Here's your first riddle," she said:

To find this place, you must erase
any thought of buildings or walls.
No mountains or stones,
not even bones,
Can touch this impressive place at all.
But when you are done,
don't dare to fiddle,
find the bottle,
it holds the next riddle.

Drew looked up from the notebook where he had written the riddle. "Does anyone have any ideas?" he asked.

"Yes," Sarah replied, "the riddle eliminates lots of places right off the bat."

"That's what I think, too," Colette said. "The first four lines say we must erase buildings, walls, mountains, stones, and bones."

"I get it," Lucia said. "That means it's not Machu Picchu..."

"God bless you," Drew said.

Lucia giggled. "No, silly," she said. "Machu Picchu is a place, not a sneeze. Anyway, we can also forget the Leaning Tower of Pisa, the Taj Mahal, the Great Wall of China, and Mt. Everest. I think the stones and bones are referring to the Giant's Causeway and the Pyramids. I think that leaves us with the Grand Canyon as the answer."

"Riddle, schmiddle," Willy said. "Are we good at this or what? I'll tell Ms. B," he said, as he bounded to the front of the plane.

Teamwork

The Jolly Jet hovered over the Grand Canyon for a few seconds before settling to the ground near the skywalk. All the kids dashed out onto the skywalk except for Drew. He got about ten feet from the edge and froze.

"Wow, this is so cool," Lucia said. "Some of the Native American tribes in this area didn't want the Hualapai Indians to build this skywalk. They said it went against their beliefs to build anything in this beautiful place."

Colette rolled her wheelchair back toward Drew. "Are you going to come out and see this?" she asked. "It's awesome. You can see all the way down to the canyon floor!"

Drew gulped. "Ahh," he said, "I think I'm okay right here."

"Drew," Colette said, "after I lost the use of my legs, I was afraid to do anything. I thought I would get hurt even worse. But my mom told me that you have to look fear in the eye and not let it get the better of you. She told me if I didn't do that, then I was truly crippled."

Colette grasped Drew's hand and placed it on the arm of her chair. "Don't let fear cripple you," she whispered. "Let's do this one step at a time. Keep looking at my eyes. Don't look down until I tell you to."

Colette rolled forward a little. Drew hesitated for a second, but then moved a step. His eyes were locked on Colette's eyes. Lucia saw what was happening and grabbed Sarah, Skylar, and Willy. They

GRAND CANYON
National park in northern Arizona
About 5,000 feet deep
Colorado River runs through bottom of it

watched silently as Drew and Colette slowly shuffled onto the skywalk.

When they reached the farthest point near the railing, Colette stopped. "Now, grab both of my arms and help me stand at the railing," she said. Drew lifted her out of the chair to the railing. He was still staring into her eyes when she said, "Look at the bald eagle swooping down into the canyon."

Drew gradually turned his head toward the canyon, and was amazed at the sight. The eagle floated along the air currents, up and down the canyon. Its wings stretched wide and its feet tucked back tightly. Its proud, white-feathered head extended way out in front.

"That's awesome!" Drew cried, an expression of wonder on his face. "Look how beautiful the colors of the canyon are! I've never seen anything like it. Pictures and movies just don't do this place justice. You have to see it for yourself!"

"It's okay for you to look down now," Colette said.

While using one hand to support Colette, Drew took a step backwards and looked down through the glass skywalk. His legs began to quiver.

"No," he thought to himself. "I won't let my fear of heights stop me from enjoying this."

"Yahoo! You're awesome, Drew! You did it! We knew you could!" Willy, Lucia, Sarah, and Skylar exclaimed, while all the other children clapped, giving Drew the **accolade** he deserved.

Colette started to slip backwards and Drew and Willy set her back in her chair. "Thank you, Colette," Drew said. "I couldn't have done this without you."

"That's why it's called teamwork," Colette replied, with a knowing smile.

Aye, Aye, Captain!

Ms. Bogus scanned over the top of the children in their orange life vests and helmets, as they stood in front of three bulky, bulbous rafts. They were about to launch on a whitewater rafting trip down the mighty Colorado River at the bottom of the Grand Canyon.

Ms. Bogus spied Drew snatch an oar from a nearby raft and poke his brother in the side with it. Skylar grabbed another oar and the two began fencing with each other.

"Boys, boys," Ms. Bogus said. "Let's save that energy for rowing your rafts, please!" Drew and Skylar put the oars back with guilty grins on their faces.

"Okay, everybody," Ms. Bogus said, after she introduced their three raft guides.

"Thomas is the lead guide, and has rafted the Colorado River more than anyone. He will be in the raft with the winners of the first riddle."

"All right!" Willy said.

"You're not coming with us?" Drew asked.

"No," Ms. Bogus said. "I will meet you with the Jolly Jet down river. Have fun!" She turned and hiked back up the hill to the Jolly Jet.

The lead raft pushed off first with the other two rafts right behind it. "Okay, kids, listen up," Thomas said. "Rafting on the Colorado River can be very dangerous, so all of you have to listen to me when I shout instructions.

"I want Drew and Skylar at the bow up front," Thomas continued. "You guys are my power strokes. When I shout 'bow dig,' you guys paddle deep and hard until I say 'stop.' Lucia and Sarah, you have the port, or left side, of the raft. Willy and Colette, you've got the starboard, or right side, of the raft."

Thomas leaned forward to get everyone's attention. "Your commands will be 'port dig,' or 'starboard dig,'" Thomas said. "If I say, 'all dig,' do you know what that means?"

"Aye, aye, Captain," Willy said. "It means we all paddle,"

"I knew you were the smart one in the bunch," Thomas said, smiling. "Follow my commands closely so we don't get into any trouble. Let's get under way!"

Thomas checked to make sure everyone was ready. "All dig slow," he shouted.

The six children began to paddle. After a lurching, uncoordinated first minute, they settled down into a rhythmic stroke.

But would all their trip go this smoothly?

Holy Cow!

"This place is awesome!" exclaimed Skylar, finally breaking the silence. "Did you guys see that coyote on the shore back there? He looked a little hungry."

"When he saw you, he figured there wasn't enough meat there to make a decent meal, so he left," Drew joked. "But you're right, this is so cool. I can't believe we're really doing this!"

The raft wobbled around a bend and started moving faster as it bounced around in the crystal-clear water. Small whitecaps peaked in front of them.

"Here it comes!" Thomas shouted.

The deafening roar of the turbulent water up ahead drowned out everything else.

Suddenly, the source of the bedlam came into view.   The raging rapids looked like they would swallow the puny raft.

"Holy cow!" Drew and Skylar both screamed, as water began to pour into the raft.

"Bow dig!" Thomas shouted.

Up, down, left, right, the raft was everywhere.

"Port dig!" Thomas yelled. The raft jerked to the left, just missing a large boulder. "Port stop!   Starboard dig!"   It lurched in the opposite direction, dodging another jagged slab of rock.   Thomas steered the raft through the **quagmire** of white foam with experienced hands.

Ten minutes later, the raft slipped into smooth water. Everyone blew out the breath they had been holding and relaxed.

"That was the best!" Willy shouted. "You guys did great," he said to Drew and Skylar. "Didn't they, Captain?"

"Yep," Thomas said.   "You guys will be pros by the time we get through the next five sets of rapids."

"Five?" Skylar exclaimed. "Oh, man! My arms are killing me already."

Three hours later, the raft floated around the final bend in the river.

"Congratulations!" Thomas said. "You all did a great job! I've had groups of kids older than you who only made it past the second set of rapids." Thomas turned and noticed that the other two rafts were nowhere in sight. "In fact, you're the only group of children your age to ever make it through all the rapids."

"Teamwork!" they all shouted with tired glee.

Colette noticed a bottle floating in the water near the riverbank. "Skylar, scoop up that bottle," she said. "Maybe it has a message inside!"

Skylar plunged his hand into the icy water and yanked the green, glass bottle from the river.

"Look!" Colette said. "There's another shiny metal tube inside. I'll bet it has a note in it. It's a riddle in a bottle!"

"Let's wait to open it until we're all onboard the Jolly Jet," Ms. Bogus said, suddenly appearing on the riverbank. "Then we can read the riddle so everyone has a chance to solve it."

"I wonder what it says!" Lucia said. "I love surprises!"

Brains Over Brawn

When the rafters arrived at the Jolly Jet, the rest of the children were already there. They had all been too tired to finish the course.

"Isn't it time to open the bottle?" Lucia asked.

"Open the bottle! Open the bottle!" The class began to cheer.

Ms. Bogus popped the cork off the bottle and removed the tube. She turned the tube upside down and shook it. Another ancient-looking scroll fell into her hand.

"Okay," Ms. Bogus said. "Break up into your groups and write this down."

Finn MacCool had a plan
to battle the man,
His greatest rival across the sea.
The challenge he laid,
could not be delayed,
'Til he saw his rival was larger
than he.
You'll find your next fate,
at the site of a gate,
Just off the path,
in a hollow that faces the sea.

"Finn MacCool?" Skylar said. "That's an awesome name, but who is he?"

"It sounds like an Irish name," Sarah guessed. "So maybe this has something to do with the Giant's Causeway?"

"It does," said Lucia. "Finn MacCool was a mythical giant who roamed the north coast of Northern Ireland. He would stand on the shore and look across the sea to Scotland. He was looking for his rival, a Scottish giant named Benandonner. One day, he decided to challenge him to a battle to decide who was the strongest."

"Is this going to be like the story about Paul Bunyan and his ox tearing up the land to make the Great Lakes?" Willy asked. "But instead, their battle made the causeway?"

"Oh, no," Lucia said. "It's nothing like that. There were no boats big enough to carry a giant, so Finn built the causeway out of large basalt stones. That way, the Scottish giant could walk over on dry land. But when Finn got a good look at him, he knew Benandonner was larger and meaner than he had thought."

"Okay," Willy said. "This is one of those bully stories where the bully gets his comeuppance, right?"

"No, Willy," Lucia said. "Please, stop interrupting. So, Finn went back to hide in his house where his wife disguised him as a baby. She stuffed him in a big cradle she had quickly made. She told him he had to pretend he was asleep, no matter what."

The kids stared at Lucia, spellbound by her story. "When Benandonner came into the house," Lucia continued, "Finn's wife told him that Finn wasn't there and asked him not to wake Finn's son. Once he saw how huge Finn's baby was, he said he didn't want to tangle with Finn. In fact, he was so scared he fled the house and tore the Causeway apart so Finn wouldn't follow him back to Scotland."

"Ha!" Willy said. "Finn sounds like my kind of guy. If you can't beat them with your brawn, beat them with your brains."

"Yeah," Colette said, "but in this case, it was his wife who had the brains. I'll go tell Ms. B we have the answer to the riddle."

Follow Me, If You Can

As the Jolly Jet swooped low over the Giant's Causeway, Lucia started bouncing up and down in her seat. "Oh my gosh!" she shouted. "Look at those incredible stone columns!"

Drew jumped across the aisle and pressed his nose against the window. "They look like a bunch of giant stepping stones," he said.

"The Giant's Causeway is made up of layers of rock," Lucia said. "Experts think that volcanoes erupted and molten rock poured into a watery depression in the ground. It created steam, which bubbled up through the bottom of the lava, leaving thousands of columns of basalt."

"Salt?" asked Drew. "It sure doesn't look like the salt on my dinner table."

Lucia giggled. "*Basalt*," she said. "It's a type of rock."

The Jolly Jet landed on the water and floated on its pontoons right up to a set of hexagonal stepping stones that led to a path. One by one, the kids leaped off the aircraft's ramp and onto the Giant's Causeway.

"Goodbye!" Ms. Bogus called. "Follow the clues and I'll be waiting here when you get back."

Willy led his group over several piles of stones. "Check this out," he said. "It looks like a king's throne." Willy sat down and spread his arms out on the "armrests" of the throne.

GIANT'S CAUSEWAY
Basalt rock formations in Northern Ireland
About 40,000 columns
Look like "stepping stones"

"It's called the Wishing Chair," Lucia said.

"Really?" Willy asked. "Well then, I'll make a wish." He closed his eyes and held his hands out in front of him, palms up.

"I'm wishing for a bag of cheeseburgers to fall into my hands," Willy said slowly. "I'm getting really hungry. Are there any Irish restaurants around here where we can get some corned beef and cabbage or Shepherd's pie?"

"I wish," replied Skylar. "Hey, let's play 'follow the leader.'"

"Okay," Willy agreed. "I'm the leader!"

Willy clambered over the wishing chair and jumped across two rows of stones. He landed hard and almost slid off the end of another stone. As Drew and Skylar followed him, he skidded down a leaning column perched like a playground slide.

When Willy reached the bottom, Lucia was standing there with her hands on her hips and a scowl on her face. "This is not a playground," she said. "Look around you. This is something to admire. You're not

supposed to treat it like a jungle gym. Besides, we have to solve this clue before the other two groups do."

"That's easy," Willy said. "The riddle says it's at the site of a gate. We just have to look for a gate. Maybe there's one by a cafeteria or a visitor's center. That makes me hungry again," he added, rubbing his stomach.

"I don't think that's the kind of gate the riddle means," Sarah said.

"I agree," Colette said. "I remember reading something about a gate made out of these basalt columns when we were doing our research in the library. You guys remember that, don't you?" Colette looked at the three boys. "Oh, then again, maybe you were too busy shooting spitballs at people."

"You're right, Colette," Lucia said. "The gate the riddle refers to is called the Giant's Gate, and it's just down that path over there." She pointed to a gravel pathway leading up to the green, mossy cliffs.

The group fell in place behind Lucia as she trudged up the path to the gate.

"The riddle says we'll find our next fate, just off the path, in a hollow that faces the sea," Drew said. "What's a hollow?"

"Don't you remember Winnie the Pooh?" Willy asked. "I think the owl slept in a hollow in a tree, so it must be some type of hole."

"Maybe one of the stone columns has a hollow," Skylar suggested, "because I don't see any trees close by."

Colette clutched a large rock and started to thump each column as she rolled by it.

TING! TING! TING! **THUNK!**

"I think I found it!" Colette shouted. As she reached along the side of the column, she felt a hollow, then a small, smooth metal tube inside it. "I've got the next clue, too!" she cried.

Strap On Your Shoes

After finding the next clue, Lucia and Sarah finally gave in and played tag among the stepping stones. Before leaving, the kids gazed out to the glistening sea one last time, and inhaled the fresh, clean air.

"I'll always remember this place," Sarah said softly. Lucia nodded her head in silent ageement.

As the class climbed aboard the Jolly Jet, Colette handed the tube to Ms. Bogus.

"Are you going to tell us the riddle now?" Lucia asked.

"Sure," Ms. Bogus replied. "Break up into your groups and get your pens fired up, because here it is." She unrolled the scroll.

The site that you seek,
is not for the weak,
So strap on your walking shoes.
Don't look to the west,
while you're on this quest,
Or you'll miss the watchtower
at Mutianyu.
Much is not more,
when you walk in the door,
So look at a vase,
to find your next place.

"This has got to be the hardest one so far," Sarah said. "I have no idea what it's talking about."

"What do you think, Lucia?" Colette asked.

"Well," Lucia answered, "I think we should use the process of elimination again. The riddle says to strap on your walking shoes. I think that eliminates the Taj Mahal, the Leaning Tower, and Mt. Everest because you probably wouldn't do a lot of walking at any of them."

"You don't think you'd do a lot of walking at Mt. Everest?" Skylar asked.

"No," Lucia replied, "you would do a lot of climbing, so you would need special mountain climber shoes."

"That leaves the Great Wall, the Pyramids, and Machu Picchu," Willy said.

Drew was about to say "God bless you" when Willy cut him off. "Don't even think of it, Drew," he warned. Drew shut his mouth. "The Pyramids and Machu Picchu don't have any watchtowers, but I remember seeing a picture of the Great Wall and it does, right?"

"Yes it does, Willy," Lucia said.

"Great," Colette said. "But the wall is 4,000 miles long. How do we know what part of the wall to go to?"

"The riddle says 'don't look to the west,'" Skylar said. "So it must be a watchtower in the east."

Lucia snapped her fingers. "I've got it!" she said. "I just remembered something from the travel book I was reading when you shot that spitball at me, Willy."

"Ahh, sorry," Willy said.

"That's okay," Lucia said. "I had fun getting you back. The Great Wall goes right by the northern side of the city of Beijing, which is a city in the east. It's also one of the most popular places for tourists to visit the wall. Near Beijing is a place called..."

"Mutianyu!" everyone but Willy shouted. "God bless you?" he said.

Your Wish Is My Command

The Jolly Jet plunged out of the sky and zipped over the northern part of Beijing, China's capital city. "There it is!" Lucia shouted. She gasped at the sight of the endless, man-made, rock and brick wall that almost stretched across the entire country.

"When you look at it from above," Drew said, "it looks like a snake."

"Snake! Where's a snake?" Colette said, snatching a quick glance around her feet.

"Get real, Colette," Willy said. "You know there aren't any snakes on this plane."

"Look down below," Drew said. "I meant that the Great Wall looks like a snake."

Colette breathed a big sigh of relief. "Willy, why didn't you say that in the first place?"

"Uhh," Drew said. "I thought I did."

The Jolly Jet landed with a soft thud not far from the path leading to the wall. "Okay, children," Ms. Bogus said. "Be back here in two hours."

The kids sprinted toward the Great Wall. Drew pushed Colette's chair up a ramp next to a staircase.

"Thanks for helping me," Colette said.

"No problem," Drew panted, as he watched most of his classmates run toward the larger of the two towers on either side of them. He turned and saw Lucia, Willy, Skylar, and Sarah climbing the stairs to the top of the smaller tower.

Great Wall of China

Rock wall built 2,000 years ago

Almost 4,000 miles long

Defended China from invading armies

"Drew, Colette!" Lucia shouted, waving at them. "Come on up here."

Drew moved Colette's wheelchair over to the bottom of the tower staircase. "Are you game for this?" he asked.

She looked at the stack of stairs before them. "I think the question is, are *you* game for this?" Colette asked.

"Sure," Drew said. "You're light as a feather. It's your chair that's heavy. Let's do it!"

A few minutes later, they stood on the top of the tower, looking out at the incredible length of the wall. It stretched endlessly in both directions.

"Come on, man," Willy said. "I thought you two would never get up here."

"What's the rush?" Drew asked.

"There's a couple of guys rapelling down the tower and they said they'd let us try it," Willy said.

"We didn't want to go without you guys," Lucia said. "So let's get all harnessed up."

"Hold it!" Colette said. "So, what is rapelling, exactly?"

"It's what they call it when you climb down a cliff or a building with ropes," Willy said. "It's so much fun!"

Drew and Colette waited as their friends went down first. Finally, the man controlling the ropes turned to them. "I see you in wheelchair," he remarked. "You can no go down by self. Must go with him. Okay?" the man said, pointing at Drew.

"Sure," Colette said. "I wouldn't miss this for anything."

The man took an extra rope and wrapped it around a support column. He clipped a metal ring, called a carabiner clip, to the rope itself. He then secured Colette to Drew's back and told him what to do next.

Drew looked out over the edge. For a second he thought of backing out. "I won't let fear control my life," he thought.

Drew positioned himself and leaned back slightly. He released the rope and they dropped a foot. He tightened it quickly.

Colette hung out over the ground below. She looked down. "Oh, boy!" she said. "Maybe we should rethink this?"

Drew pushed off the ledge and released the rope lock.

"**Aaahhh!**" Colette screamed.

Drew released and tightened the rope as he worked his way down the wall in leaping steps, keeping his legs straight out in front of him. The whole trip down the tower took less than a minute. When they landed, Colette thumped Drew on the back of his head. "I wasn't ready to go yet," she grumbled.

"I wasn't ready to go when you took me out on the skywalk, either," Drew said, smiling.

Colette smiled back. "Let's do it again!"

After going up and down the wall several more times, Willy gathered everyone together. "Hey guys," he said, "look!" Willy pointed at a group of kids over by the large tower.

"That's Johnny's group," Lucia said. "They're looking for the scroll!"

Much Is Not More

"Fun time is over," Lucia said. "As my mom says, it's time to get serious." She yanked the riddle out of her pocket and read the last two lines. "'Much is not more, when you walk in the door. So look at a vase, to find your next place.'"

"I don't get what it means by 'much is not more,'" Skylar said.

"I think I do," Sarah said. "It's like when you look at two things and because one is larger or prettier than the other, you think it contains something special or something more. But then you find out that the smaller or less beautiful item was actually the better one."

"I get what you mean, Sarah," Lucia said, looking at the two towers they stood between.

"The larger of the two towers seems like the logical place to look for the scroll."

"But," Drew continued Lucia's thought, "the smaller tower may have the 'more' we're looking for."

They all scurried back up the ramp and burst through the small tower's doorway.

"Whoa!" Willy said, looking around the small, sparsely furnished room. "If this is 'more,' I hate to think what 'much' was."

The room contained an old wooden table, a couple of chairs, and one picture on the wall.

"Everyone spread out and look for the vase," Lucia said. "It must be hidden."

"Hey, there's a vase in this picture," Skylar said, pointing at the painting on the wall.

"Good find," Willy commented. "But I don't think we can pull the scroll out of a picture."

"Hey, maybe it's behind the picture," Colette suggested.

Skylar lifted the picture off the wall and turned it over. Sure enough, a metal tube was taped to the bottom of the frame.

"We're getting pretty good at this," Skylar said. "We could be in a detective movie, or even start our own detective agency."

"Don't get too far ahead of yourself, Sherlock," Lucia advised with a wink. "Confucius say, 'Things going well can always go wrong!'"

Just Call Me Sherlock

"Open the tube!" shouted Drew.

The three groups huddled together in the Jolly Jet's cabin, waiting for Ms. Bogus to read the next riddle.

She peered at the class over her cat-eye glasses. "Johnny, where do you hope we are going next?" she asked.

"I think Mt. Everest would be cool or that Inca place, Machu Picchu," he replied.

"God bless you," Drew said, causing a few giggles in the class.

"That's getting a little old," Willy said.

"Okay," Drew said. "That was the last time."

"Here's the riddle," Ms. Bogus said.

This is the place,
that you must not chase
Each other 'round the gardens
for fun.
Respect the dead,
encased in a marble bed,
And you'll find your guess
is the proper one.
For the next one on your list,
the left tower you must not miss,
If it's the item you desire, look at
the gilded spire.

"It's the Taj Mahal!" Lucia shouted, covering her mouth with her hand. "Ahh, sorry. I got a little excited there."

"Why do you think it's the Taj Mahal?" Ms. Bogus asked.

"I know it's the Taj Mahal," Lucia said.

"Because it is the only wonder with a gilded spire on each of its domes. Also, the Taj, as people like to call it, has more than one watchtower."

"Very good!" Ms. Bogus said. "Your group is now four for four."

"Okay, Lucia," Skylar said. "I think we ought to be calling *you* Sherlock, not me."

Pizza on My Mind

"I thought the Taj Mahal gardens were beautiful, but can you believe how gorgeous the building is?" Lucia asked, as she walked next to Colette.

Colette stared, speechless, at the stunning, white marble monument, part of a vast complex including lush gardens, sparkling reflecting pools, and a sacred mosque.

"I am just amazed," Colette said finally. "No wonder this is considered a wonder of the world. It's just so...perfect!"

"I think the domes are its most beautiful feature," Sarah added. "They catch your eye immediately."

"This place is pretty cool," Willy said. "I had wondered what the big deal was about somebody's tomb before we got here, but now I see. I really like those gardens. Everything is perfectly in place!"

Willy's stomach growled. "I'll tell you what, though," he said. "Right now, a real thing of beauty would be one of those Chicago deep dish pizzas I had this past summer in the Windy City."

"You and your stomach," Lucia said. "Let's stay on task!

"It's not just the Taj Mahal's beauty that I like," she added. "I also love its history. Did you know that Emperor Shah Jahan had the Taj Mahal built as a tomb for his second wife, Mumtaz Mahal, a Muslim Persian princess? She died giving birth to their fourteenth child in 1631."

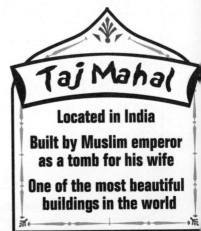

Taj Mahal

Located in India

Built by Muslim emperor as a tomb for his wife

One of the most beautiful buildings in the world

"Hold it!" Skylar said. "You mean there's a body in there?"

"Yes," Lucia said, "at least what's left of it after almost 400 years!"

"That's cool!" Skylar said. "But it's time to solve the riddle, so we can find the next location."

Sarah slid the riddle out of her pocket. "'For the next one on your list, the left tower you must not miss. If it's the item you desire, look at the gilded spire.' This is pretty simple, because all the domes are topped with gilded or gold painted spires."

"Good," Willy said. "Then let's go to the one on the left dome. I saw some stairs over this way. Follow me."

Willy worked his way through the crowd of tourists to the staircase. The kids bolted up several flights of stairs until they reached the top level. Willy stopped suddenly. "I don't believe it," he said. "Johnny's group beat us up here!"

"*AAHHHHHHH!*" A piercing scream filled the air.

"Help! Please help us!" a frantic female voice shouted.

Boys! They Never Listen

Willy raced to the tower's balcony. Lee, a tall, thin classmate, was hanging off the balcony, more than 100 feet above the ground. Johnny was struggling to hold onto the back of his belt.

Willy and Drew helped Johnny drag Lee back onto the balcony. "What were you trying to do? Get yourself killed?" Willy asked, exasperated. "Oh, boy," he added. "Now I'm starting to sound like my father."

Lee collapsed on the balcony next to Johnny. "We were trying to get the next clue off the dome before you guys did," Johnny said, panting. "But Lee lost his grip and slipped off the balcony ledge."

"I tried to tell them that they should find a pole or something to reach up and knock it loose," Sin Ging, one of the girls in Johnny's group, said. "But you know boys. They never listen!"

"Tell me about it," Lucia said, looking at Willy.

"Here's a pole right here," Sarah said. "Get ready to catch it." She stretched to place the pole over the top of the dome and tapped a small, decorative round box. It slid off the dome into Drew's hands.

"I got it," Drew said. He opened it, saw the metal tube inside, and shut it quickly. "Yesssss!" he exclaimed.

Johnny frowned. "Beat again," he mumbled.

Drew looked at Johnny. "I believe this is yours," he said, handing the box over to Johnny. "You guys beat us here fair and square."

Johnny stood up. "Thanks!" he said.

A Man's Got To Eat

The Jolly Jet climbed through the sky as Ms. Bogus addressed the children.

"Well," Ms. Bogus said, "I hope all of you have learned a valuable lesson here. Never desire something so much that you don't think before you act. Remember, the decisions you make dictate the life you lead. Unfortunately, many people have to learn this simple fact the hard way. Don't be one of them."

The kids pounced on the boxed lunches Ms. Bogus had set out for them.

"Ms. B," Willy said, "do you have another one of these? I'm still hungry."

"I'm sorry, Willy," Ms. Bogus said. "But I only brought one each."

Lucia shoved her box over to Willy. "Here," she said. "You can have the rest of mine."

"Hey, Willy," Drew said. "Maybe the next riddle will be about the Leaning Tower of Pisa. Then we could stop and get some 'pisa' to eat," he giggled. "Get it? Pisa, pizza."

"Don't go joking with a man's stomach," Willy warned.

"Okay," Ms. Bogus said. "Here's the next riddle."

> Fly high into the air,
> see a sight that's very rare.
> The highest spot in all the land,
> you'll find snow but never sand.
> The stars and stripes are at the peak,
> find the right one for what you seek.

"That's easy," Johnny said. "It's got to be Mt. Everest."

"Very good, Johnny," Ms. Bogus said. "And because you figured it out, you get to take half of your team and half of Lucia's team up to the peak!"

Plant The Flag

The Jolly Jet hovered over a flat area at the top of Mt. Everest, creating a mini blizzard. Johnny, Lee, Sin Ging, Lucia, Willy, and Drew jumped off the ramp in their snowsuits, oxygen tanks strapped to their backs. Separate ropes, with carabiner clips at each end, connected each of their climbing harnesses to the person in front of them. They walked together silently, because the oxygen masks made it difficult to talk.

Johnny stopped to stare in awe at the spectacular view. The azure blue sky was more vivid than he had ever seen before, as was the blinding white snow, which blanketed every mountaintop around them.

He lifted his mask. "Can you believe we're at the top of the world?" he asked.

"Yep," Drew replied, spreading his arms wide. "How cool is this? Just look at that view. There's nothing like it. People can try all they want to duplicate Mother Nature, but she'll always outdo us."

"Does anybody have any ideas on where to look?" Sin Ging asked, interrupting their reverie.

"First things first," Willy said, attempting to dance in the thick snow, but ending up flat on his back. "I told you I would do a little dance on Mt. Everest," he said, roaring with laughter.

Drew held up a small flag with the Alpine McAlpine school logo on it. "I hereby claim this mountain for the Alpine

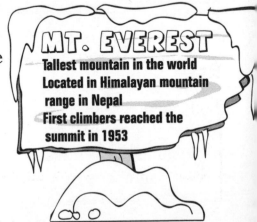

MT. EVEREST
Tallest mountain in the world
Located in Himalayan mountain range in Nepal
First climbers reached the summit in 1953

McAlpine school district," he announced. "This is one small step for Alpine kids, and one large step for kids all over the world!"

Drew tried to stick the flag in the ground, but it was frozen solid. He piled a bunch of rocks around the flag instead.

"That was cool," Johnny said. "I wish I had thought of that."

"Does anyone remember the last line of the riddle?" Drew asked. "It's cold out here and I don't want to end up like so many climbers who froze to death on this big rock."

"I memorized it," Lucia said. "'The stars and stripes are at the peak, find the right one for what you seek.' The stars and stripes are the American flag."

They all turned and gazed at the many flags flying at the top of Mt. Everest. A handful of American flags were scattered around. "Okay, I see several American flags, but which one is the right one?" Willy asked.

"The one on the right, silly," Lucia said.

The shivering children trudged over to the flag rippling in the fierce wind. "I don't see anything here," Johnny said.

"Me neither," Drew agreed. "Maybe it's one of the other flags."

"No," Willy said, "it's this one. See this pile of rocks? They're all the same except for that one there." He pointed at a black rock. "That's a piece of lava rock, which you wouldn't normally find at this altitude."

Lucia lifted the rock. Sunlight gleamed off the shiny metal tube underneath it.

"We got it!" she cried. "Now, let's get out of here! I'm freeeeezing!"

"You're the lead man, Johnny," Drew said, trying to sound like his dad. "Take us back to some nice, warm airplane seats."

Johnny took two steps. Suddenly, the snow beneath his feet crumbled. He started sliding down the mountain! The ten feet of slack rope between Johnny and Lee tightened, yanking Lee off his feet and down the hill after him.

"**AAAHHH!**" Sin Ging screamed, knowing she was next.

Dig In!

"Willy!" Drew shouted. "Dig in with your heels!" Drew unclipped the carabiner that connected the rope between his climbing harness and Willy's harness. He ran around a tall but narrow boulder. As he came around the boulder, he clipped the carabiner to the rope he'd wound around the boulder, just like the man at the Great Wall of China had done when they were rapelling down the tower.

As Sin Ging slid down the hill after Lee, Willy wrapped his arms around Lucia's waist, fell back, and dug the heels of his climbing boots into the snow. Lucia's rope became taut, and the weight of the three other kids started to pull her and Willy slowly through the snow.

Willy knew that the kids sliding down the mountain needed to get hooked up to the boulder to stop their fall. He reached back and unclipped the carabiner from his harness, which attached him to the rope around the boulder. He quickly clipped it to the carabiner that connected Lucia's harness to Sin Ging's harness. The rope snapped tight, stopping the kids' downward slide just as they were about to plummet over the edge. "Whew—that was close!" Willy shouted.

Drew tied off a safety line to feed down to Johnny, Lee, Sin Ging, and Lucia. "That was quick thinking, Willy," he said.

"Thanks—you, too," Willy replied, panting.

"Hey guys," Drew shouted. "Grab the safety line and climb back up."

"Yeah," Willy shouted. "And hurry up! I'm starting to get REALLY c-c-c-cold!"

We Don't Want To Go Home

The climbers chattered excitedly with their classmates about their adventure while sipping steaming hot chocolate in the Jolly Jet.

"Willy and Drew were awesome," Lucia said. "Their quick thinking really got us out of a jam."

"It was a good thing we had just gone rapelling so you guys knew how to use the equipment you had," Colette asked.

Ms. Bogus shook her head. "I don't know," she said. "This trip seems to be getting more dangerous with every stop. Maybe we should head back now."

"Come on, Ms. B," Lucia begged. "Everything will be fine." She turned toward the three groups. "Everyone who wants to continue, raise your hands."

Every hand in the class shot into the air. Willy threw up both of his hands.

"Okay," Ms. Bogus said. "But if we run into any more trouble, the trip is over. You'll all have to learn about the world from your desks like every other student at Alpine."

"Deal," Lucia said. "So, what's the next riddle?"

"I thought you'd never ask, Lucia," Ms. Bogus said, smiling. The class giggled.

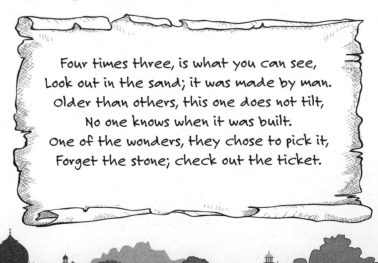

Four times three, is what you can see,
Look out in the sand; it was made by man.
Older than others, this one does not tilt,
No one knows when it was built.
One of the wonders, they chose to pick it,
Forget the stone; check out the ticket.

All the kids looked at each other, waiting for someone to shout out the answer. When no one did, they started talking in their groups.

"I think it's the Pyramids," Lucia said. "Four times three represents the four triangle sides of the Pyramid. Plus, it's out in the sand, and it's made by man. Plus, it doesn't tilt."

"It says it's older than others," Willy said. "That must mean the Great Pyramid of Giza, because they don't really know how old it is."

"I thought they knew how old the Great Pyramid was," Colette said.

"Nope!" Sarah said. "Some scientists think it was built during the reign of a pharaoh named Khufu, about 2500 BC, but a lot of other scientists think it's older than that."

"I've read that when it comes to the past, it's all guesswork," Skylar said. "Because we aren't seeing the past, we're seeing something from the past in the present."

"That's right," Sarah said, standing up. "I'll go give Ms. Bogus our best guess for this riddle. Ancient Egypt—here we come!"

Bunch Of Chickens

The black, angry clouds looked like they were going to explode upon the children any minute. Lightning lit the sky.

BOOOMMM!

Thunder rolled across the sky, rattling the ground beneath their feet. The kids were stumped. They had already spent more time at this wonder than any of the previous ones. They had roamed around the Great Pyramid of Giza and three smaller Pyramids several times, trying to find their clue.

The children stood at the Pyramid's entrance, confused and discouraged.

Willy peered at the Great Pyramid of Giza and scratched his head. "I think we're going to have to go inside to solve the riddle's last two lines. I don't think the clue is out here."

"We can't," Sarah said. "It's closed to the public."

Drew stole a glance around them. No one else was there, just the six of them. "Hey," he said. "Everyone else must have given up and gone back to the plane to stay dry. What a bunch of chickens, afraid of a little wind and rain."

"Come on," Willy said. "Let's see if the guard will let us look around inside." He raced to the entrance. Everyone followed except Colette.

BOOOMMM!

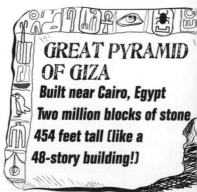

GREAT PYRAMID OF GIZA
Built near Cairo, Egypt
Two million blocks of stone
454 feet tall (like a
48-story building!)

Colette was busy checking how close together the giant blocks of limestone and basalt were placed. And some people think

that people from the past weren't as smart as us, she thought. She didn't hear her friends leave because of the crashing thunder.

As the group entered the Pyramid, they looked around for a guard, but couldn't find one. "I guess that means we can look around all we want," Willy said, moving forward.

"How in the world did they build these things, anyway?" Drew asked, looking around at the huge blocks of stone.

"No one knows for sure," Skylar said. "But some experts think the Egyptians hauled stones up ramps with ropes. They say it may have taken 10 or 20 years to build the Great Pyramid."

"*AAAHHHH!*" A desperate scream interrupted their conversation.

Snakes and Storms

"Who was that?" Skylar asked.

"It was Colette!" Drew shouted. "She's still outside!"

The kids stumbled over each other to get back outside.

BOOOOMM! BOOOOMM!

Lightning streaked across the sky, and thunder roared in their ears.

"Where is she?" Skylar shouted.

Drew spotted Colette. Her wheelchair was backed up against the wall of the Pyramid. Something was moving at her feet.

"Oh, no!" Sarah screamed. "That's a snake—I think it's a sand viper!"

"Somebody help me!" Colette pleaded softly, trying not to alarm the snake.

"Just stay calm," Drew said, turning toward Skylar and Willy. "We need a weapon to kill it."

"Hold it," Colette said shakily. "I have a weapon." She took a deep breath, and slowly backed her chair a few inches away from the snake. Then, she quickly whipped her chair forward. The front wheel rolled over the viper's head, crushing it.

"That was awesome, Colette!" Drew said. Sarah and Lucia ran to Colette and hugged her tight.

"You're the man, I mean, woman!" Willy said. "Now let's get back inside the Pyramid."

"Willy," Drew said, "it's too dark in there. We need flashlights to find anything."

"No, we don't," Lucia said.

"Well," Willy said. "The quiet one finally speaks."

"I'm sorry," Lucia said. "I've just been trying to figure out the riddle. I'm pretty sure I know the answer, and it's not in there."

"What's the answer?" Colette asked, sliding her chair away from the dead viper.

"The next riddle is at the ticket office," Lucia said. "The riddle says, 'One of the wonders, they chose to pick it. Forget the stone; check out the ticket.' It means that if you choose to look at the Great Pyramid more closely, you need to buy a ticket. It tells us to forget the stones themselves."

"Like I said," Skylar remarked, "you're the real Sherlock Holmes."

Just then, huge sheets of rain poured onto the Egyptian desert. The fierce wind blew it sideways. "Come on!" Lucia shouted. "Last one to the ticket office is a wet noodle!"

The children screamed and squealed as they ran through the stinging rain. An Egyptian lady sat behind the screened-in counter at the ticket office.

"Uhh," Lucia said. "Do you have anything you're supposed to give to some kids, if they ask for it?"

The lady reached behind her and grabbed a familiar-looking metal tube. She handed it to Lucia without saying a word.

"Thank you," Lucia said, clutching the tube tightly. She squinted at the drenching rain. "Okay, only two more to go," she said. "Lead the way, Willy!"

Willy bolted toward the Jolly Jet, trying to hit every puddle with a **SPLASH!** along the way.

I'm Starving

After drying themselves off with warm, fluffy towels, the children joined the rest of the class in the Jolly Jet.

"Okay, children," Ms. Bogus said. "We're getting down to the last two wonders. Here's your next clue."

"Please, be the Leaning Tower of Pisa," Willy said, mumbling under his breath. "I'm still hungry!"

Although this bell doesn't toll for thee,
Its beauty surpasses most, you see.
So stay together, real tight,
I hope you don't mind leaning to the right.
Its beauty as a tower cannot be beat,
Look for the cart with something to eat.

"The Leaning Tower of Pizza!" Willy shouted. "Uh! I mean Pisa."

Willy rubbed his hands together. "They have just GOT to have pizza!" he cried. "After all, it's in Italy!"

It Makes Me Dizzy

Drew and Skylar leaned their heads WAAAYYY back to get a good look at the Leaning Tower of Pisa.

"Wow!" Drew said. "It looks like it's going to fall over any minute!"

"I don't know, man!" Willy said. "It makes me dizzy just looking at it."

"Isn't it amazing?" Lucia said. "The construction of the tower began in 1173. The soil underneath it wasn't strong enough to support it, so it was already starting to sink by the time they built the third floor."

"Look at the intricate detail on all the columns," Colette said, squinting her green eyes in the bright sunlight. "I wonder why it hasn't cracked and fallen over yet."

"It was built in stages over 200 years," Lucia replied, "with several long breaks in the construction. The ground had time to settle during those breaks. Plus, it didn't crack because the tower is made of limestone, which is more flexible than rock."

"Cool," Willy said. "But how does this lead us to some pizza?"

Just then, a small cart labeled LUIGI'S PIZZA rolled up to the children.

"You kids hungry?" asked the dark-skinned, mustached man behind the cart, as he handed Willy his business card. It read, *Luigi's, Leaning Tower of Pisa, Pizza.* Willy tucked it in his shirt pocket.

"You bet!" everyone shouted. "We'll take an extra-large pepperoni pizza," Willy said.

Willy flipped open the box top and was about to grab a slice when he spied another

LEANING TOWER OF PISA
Bell tower in Pisa, Italy
Leans nearly 17 feet to the south

shiny metal tube plopped in the center of the pizza. Willy picked it up, licked off the cheese and sauce, and stuck the tube in his pocket.

"Yummmmm!" Willy said. "Tastes great! Let's dig in!"

There was only one slice of pizza left in the box when the kids returned to the Jolly Jet. Willy grabbed it. Just as he took a big, cheesy bite, Ms. Bogus read the last riddle.

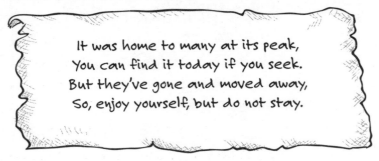

It was home to many at its peak,
You can find it today if you seek.
But they've gone and moved away,
So, enjoy yourself, but do not stay.

"This one is so easy, Ms. Bogus," Lucia said. "It's Machu Picchu."

"What's Machu Picchu, anyway?" Johnny asked.

"Machu Picchu," Lucia explained, "is a place in southern Peru. I'll tell you more about it once we get there. You just won't believe it!"

Royal Ramp

Eyes grew wide and mouths gaped open as the Jolly Jet cruised over Peru's Machu Picchu. Below, perched high on a mountaintop, was a massive complex of temples, homes, and irrigation terraces in a lush, green paradise.

"It just takes your breath away," Sarah gasped. "How did they build this? Why did they build it?" Skylar nodded his head in amazement.

Once at Machu Picchu, Lucia played the tour guide once again. "Machu Picchu," she began, "means manly peak. It was most likely a royal estate where people went for religious purposes," she explained. "It is often called the Lost City of the Incas. It was built around 1450 by an Incan ruler."

"Why was it lost?" Skylar asked.

"Few people knew about it until 1911," Lucia replied, "when an American archaeologist rediscovered it.   There are more than 100 flights of stone stairs and about 200 buildings.   Most of them are houses, but some are religious temples."

Lucia touched the side of a building with her fingertips. "Most of the buildings were made of granite blocks that were cut with bronze and smoothed with sand," she said. "They fit together so perfectly that not even the tip of a knife blade can fit b e t w e e n them."

" V e r y good, Lucia," Ms. Bogus said. "When I retire

MACHU PICCHU
Ancient city in Peru
Located on a high peak between
two mountains
Mummies found in its ruins

someday, you will be the travel agent I will use to travel the world!" She checked her watch. "You have just an hour to look around. Is that understood?"

A sea of fourth-grade heads bobbed up and down. "Okay," she said. "Have fun!"

"Hey," Skylar said, pointing up over several tiers of houses. "What's that up there?"

"That's where royalty lived," Lucia said. "These houses here were for the servants and their families."

Willy looked up and down the hill. "I bet we can get up there by following the path behind these houses."

"Do you see any ramps?" asked Colette.

Drew scooped Colette out of her chair. "We'll make our own. Let's go!"

Secret Entrance

The kids gasped for air as they struggled up the steep, grassy hill. "It's...so...hard...to...breathe," Sarah wheezed.

The boys put Colette back in her chair when they reached the top. Everyone bent over to catch their breath.

"Hey," Willy said. "That looks like an entrance over there."

"I wonder if we're allowed up here," Sarah said.

"I didn't see anything that said we couldn't go to certain areas," Lucia remarked, "so it should be okay."

The children quietly crept into a spacious room with a stone hearth and fireplace at one end, and nothing else. "Wow," Willy said.

"Check out that huge fireplace! It's so big I could walk right into it!"

Willy and Drew scrambled up onto the hearth and jumped into the area where the fire would be. "Man, I wish we had a camera," Willy said, leaning against the back wall of the fireplace. "Then you could take our pictures in here."

Suddenly, the brick under Willy's hand began to slide inward.

"What's go—" Willy yelped, as the whole back wall of the fireplace rotated, opening a two-foot-wide entrance. Willy tumbled inside.

"BILLY!" Lucia screamed.

"I'm okay," Willy shouted. "But I could sure use some light."

Drew stepped up to the opening. He stopped at the edge to look inside, motioning to the other kids to join him.

Inside the secret entrance, a torch next to Drew lit up on its own, as did several other torches around the room. Willy stood in the

center of the room, his arms flailing around his head.

"Cobwebs!" Willy said. "I hate cobwebs!" He suddenly noticed the light, and the wide-eyed look on everyone's faces.

"What?" Willy said.

Skylar pointed over Willy's shoulder. He whirled around. Massive, elegant thrones lined the far wall. Sitting in the chairs were the mummified remains of the royal family—hidden for centuries! Dusty jewelry hung from their necks and wrapped around their arms and legs.

"Mummies!" Willy cried. "This just keeps getting better!"

"I wonder how much that jewelry is worth?" Sarah asked.

Lucia stepped forward, just missing stepping on a gold square plate embedded in the floor in front of the corpse of a young girl. She leaned in to take a closer look. "Look at how straight her teeth are," she said. "I wish my teeth were that straight." As she leaned

in a little closer, spiders climbed out of the young mummy's mouth, nose, and ears.

"AAAHHH!" Lucia screamed. As she frantically scrambled backwards, she tripped over her own feet and fell. She landed on the gold-covered square plate. It moved under her.

Whoosh! Sharp circular blades swooped down from the ceiling in opposite directions, chopping through the air where she had been standing just seconds before.

"AAAHHH!" This time all three girls screamed.

"Let's get out of here," Sarah shouted, grabbing Lucia and backing away toward the exit. Colette turned her wheelchair and unknowingly rolled over another gold plate.

WHAM! The fireplace door swung shut!

Beauty Is In The Eye Of The Beholder

"Everybody stop moving around," Willy shouted. He looked down at the floor. He could see two other gold plates strategically placed around the room. One was in front of what appeared to be the royal couple, and the other was behind them, near the back wall.

"I'm going to try something," Willy said. He picked up a rock the size of a softball and tossed it onto the plate in front of the couple. Immediately, they heard a chopping sound like helicopter blades.

"Duck!" Willy shouted. Everyone ducked except Colette. Razor sharp, flying metal discs sprang from several holes along the side walls. One disc whizzed right toward Colette. She flung herself out of her chair and fell hard onto the cold rock floor. The disc sailed across the room and smashed into the opposite wall.

"Willy!" Everyone shouted.

"Uh!" Willy said. "Sorry, Colette. Okay, there's only one trigger plate left; this time everyone stay on the floor." Willy threw another rock onto the last gold plate.

Nothing happened.

"What do we do now?" Sarah whispered.

"Wait! I hear something," Skylar observed. A grinding noise behind them became louder and louder.

"Uh, oh!" Willy cried. "Not again!"

The back wall behind the royal corpses slid to the side, revealing nothing but a dark hole beyond. Suddenly, torches began to ignite around the large interior room.

The kids crept slowly through the entrance. They stood on a balcony overlooking an immense cavern.

"Oh, my," Lucia gasped, "what have we found?"

The torchlights gleamed off a massive pile of glowing gold coins and sparkling jewels. "Wowwwwwww," everyone breathed.

"Willy! Drew! Lucia!" The soft voice came from beyond the fireplace.

"It's Ms. B!" Lucia shouted. All the children except Willy began to scream. "She found us! She found us!"

Willy glanced back at the treasure. "Indiana Jones, eat your heart out," he said. He stepped on the gold plate that had shut the fireplace entrance. This time, the entrance popped open.

"Hey, Ms. B," Willy said. "Did you miss us? We've been on the best fantasy field trip ever—thanks!"

Epilogue

Willy heard voices around him and opened his eyes. He was back in the classroom at Alpine McAlpine School.

"It's a tough choice between the Grand Canyon and Mt. Everest," Drew said. "But Everest was too cold for me, so I liked the Grand Canyon the best."

"I'm stuck between the Giant's Causeway and the Great Pyramid of Giza," Skylar added. "But I think I'm going to go with the Causeway because of how green everything is in Ireland. I loved that."

"Well," Lucia said, "at the start of our trip, I thought I would choose Machu Picchu because of how beautiful it is. I guess I was right, because I've never seen anything as gorgeous as that hidden treasure!"

"What did you like best about the trip, Johnny?" Ms. Bogus asked.

"Nothing," Johnny said. "I really don't think we even went on a field trip. I think it was a dream."

"You're wrong," Willy said. "It was really real, we were all there. I mean, it has to be real, we all have the same memories of what happened."

"Yeah!" the whole class shouted.

"Do all of you remember how Drew got over his fear of heights and went rapelling with Colette?" Willy asked.

"Yeah!" the whole class shouted.

"Do you remember how Colette confronted her worst fear when she crushed the head of that snake?" Willy asked.

"Yeah!" the whole class shouted again. "How about how I danced at the top of the world?" Willy asked.

"Yeah!" the whole class shouted a fourth time.

"And the best thing to remember, besides the rafting trip, was how we all worked together in our groups," Willy said. "We not only learned how to use our powers of deduction, but we learned teamwork."

"Yeah!" Everyone shouted, once again.

RRRIIIIINNNNGGG!!!   The school bell announced the end of the day.

The kids jumped out of their seats and ran to their lockers. Willy stuffed his books into his locker and noticed something in his shirt pocket. It was a business card.

Willy grinned when he read, *Luigi's, Leaning Tower of Pisa, Pizza*. "Yeah," he said, nodding his head. "We were there!"

Willy saw Drew strolling down the hall. "Hey Drew," Willy called, "you want to go get some pizza? I'm hungry!"

THE END

About the Author

Carole Marsh is an author and publisher who has written many works of fiction and non-fiction for young readers. She travels throughout the United States and around the world to research her books. In 1979 Carole Marsh was named Communicator of the Year for her corporate communications work with major national and international corporations.

Marsh is the founder and CEO of Gallopade International, established in 1979. Today, Gallopade International is widely recognized as a leading source of educational materials for every state and many countries. Marsh and Gallopade were recipients of the 2004 Teachers' Choice Award. Marsh has written more than 16 Carole Marsh Mysteries™. In 2007, she was named Georgia Author of the Year. Years ago, her children, Michele and Michael, were the original characters in her mystery books. Today, they continue the Carole Marsh Books tradition by working at Gallopade. By adding grandchildren Grant and Christina as new mystery characters, she has continued the tradition for a third generation.

Ms. Marsh welcomes correspondence from her readers. You can e-mail her at carole@gallopade.com, visit the carolemarshmysteries.com website, or write to her in care of Gallopade International, P.O. Box 2779, Peachtree City, Georgia, 30269 USA.

Talk About It!

Built-In Book Club

1. Who was your favorite character? Why?

2. What was the most exciting part of the book? Why?

3. If you could visit any of the eight wonders, which one would it be? Why?

4. The kids made fun of Ms. Bogus before they met her because they heard that she was a crazy cat lady. They find out that Ms. Bogus isn't crazy at all. Discuss why you should not judge people before you meet them.

5. During their adventures, the kids help each other find the clues. Discuss why it is easier to get things done when you work with a team.

Bring it to Life!

Built-In Book Club

1. What's your wonder? Draw and describe your idea for a ninth wonder of the world! Is it a man-made place, or a natural wonder?

2. Find out more! Pick one of the eight wonders mentioned in the book that you find most interesting. Research the place and make a small model of it. Write cool facts about the place on a poster. Then, set up stations around the room for each wonder and go on a "walking tour" around the world!

3. Personality Plus! List all the characters in the book. Then, write three adjectives to describe the personality of each person. See how different people can be, and how they can work together to reach a goal!

Glossary

 accolade: an award symbolizing approval or distinction

barrage: a heavy or prolonged attack

bedlam: chaos; a state of extreme confusion or disorder

bulbous: bulging or round; shaped like a bulb

 clairvoyant: someone who can see things beyond a normal person; a psychic

comeuppance: when someone gets what they deserve, good or bad

imperative: essential or urgent

intricate: small and complex; very detailed

maelstrom: a whirlpool; or a hectic, disorderly situation

quagmire: soft, low-lying land; or a difficult situation where there seems to be no easy way out

spellbound: when something holds your attention completely; fascinated

turbulent: violently agitated or disturbed

**Hey, Kids! Visit
www.carolemarshmysteries.com to:**

- Join the Carole Marsh Mysteries Fan Club!

- Write one sensational sentence using all five SAT words in the glossary!

- Download an Eight Wonders Word Search!

- Take a Pop Quiz!

- Download a Scavenger Hunt!

- Learn Fascinating Facts about the Eight Wonders!